GREEK
& ROMAN
MYTHOLOGY

GREEK & ROMAN MYTHOLOGY

MALCOM COUCH

TODTRI

ISBN 1-57717-064-4

Visit us on the web!

www.todtri.com

This book was designed and produced by Todtri Book Publishers
P.O. Box 572, New York, NY 10116-0572 FAX: (212) 695-6984

e-mail:todtri@mindspring.com

Author: Simon Goodenough

Publisher: Robert M. Tod
Editor: Nicolas Wright
Art Director: Ron Pickless
Designer: Vic Giolitto
Typeset and DTP: Blanc Verso/UK

Printed and bound in Singapore

Contents

Introduction

What is mythology? Is it, quite simply, tales which have arisen from earlier cultures about the adventures and lives of former heroes and gods? Or is it an attempt to perpetuate allegorical tales which bear a definite moral or scientific explanation for the creation of the world, the reason for our life, and for what might happen after death?

Probably a bit of both. In addition to the abiding love we have had over the centuries for the original tales of Greek and Roman mythology, it is important to remember that the original tales refer to a time far distant from our own. The nature of life, and even the topography of earth, was very different from what we know today. The stories ascribe human characteristics to larger-than-life characters

and their deeds and actions often destroy all sense of time and place. Yet, above all, the tales were planned for enjoyment, instruction, and wonder.

In that respect this book is a much shorter version of the full tales. It is only a brief resume of those adventures and events which were originally written down for "public" consumption. It will, hopefully, act as an introduction for those who wish to know more, or as a quick easy-style reference for those who do not need a fuller retelling of the original stories.

All that follows comes either from the writings of Hesiod and the works ascribed to Homer; from the retelling of those tales over nearly two thousand years by writers, poets, and dramatists; and from those bite-sized chunks of information on the subject which we all have seen, read, and heard.

The Greeks and the Romans

To say that the Greeks came before the Romans is to state an obvious historical fact. However, it is important to realize that without the tales commonly referred to as Greek mythology then what we now refer to as Roman mythology would be completely different.

The Greek writer Hesiod produced the *Theogony*, a complete work outlining the origin of the world and the genealogies of the gods. As such, it contained a rather dauntingly long list of who-gave-birth-to-who, who-lived-with-who, and who-spent-the-night-with-who. But Hesiod certainly succeeded in establishing the history of the gods for future reading.

Many of the gods who were originally worshiped in Greece came from previous

Right: An Edwardian depiction of one of the many almost daily duties of Roman life: sacrificing to the Lares, the gods of hearth and home.

cultures in the near and even further East. But the effect of Greek mythology was such that these tales have persisted within western experience. With our greater knowledge of science and evolution we might find the ancient understanding of the universe hard to believe, but it is an integral part of Greek and Roman mythology.

The ancient Greeks believed the earth was flat and shaped like a circle with their land occupying the middle. In the center of this land lay Mount Olympus, the home of the gods, and a little farther away was Delphi, the navel of the earth. Just below both, and crossing the earth from east to west, was the great dividing sea.

Further to the north and east of Greece lay the lands of the Hyperboreans, a region full of bliss and jollity and divided from Greece by a mountain range from which the North Wind came. South of the great sea lived the Ethiopians, who lived happily and knew no wars. Westward lay the Isles of the Blessed, a fortunate place where only those who had pleased the gods could reside and where there was everlasting bliss. Circling all these land masses was the great ocean stream, outlining the edge of the world.

The Greeks knew nothing of what lay beyond what they had knowledge of, and their world, therefore, was very enclosed. The only other dominion that interested the Greeks was the sky, which explains why so many of their tales feature the stars and constellations.

Roman mythological characters were not simply stolen from Greek mythology but were a natural progression. The history of Greece included expansion. Greek

Above: Greek myths and legends played a major part in early Italian life. This was a direct result of the early colonization of Southern Italy, Sicily, and Southern France by the Greeks. One of the main centers for Greek worship in Sicily was the magnificent temple of Agrigento in Sicily.

Following pages: According to Greek mythology, 9,570-foot-high Mount Olympus in Northern Greece was the home of the ancient gods and from where they played with the lives of mere earthbound mortals.

9

communities and tribes populated Sicily and parts of Southern Italy. As what we now call the Roman world developed, there was a natural inclusion of the folktales, music, and poetry which had emanated from classical Greece. The genius of Greece was in philosophy, literature, the arts, and science. The Romans excelled in industry, warfare, and government.

In nearly all cases the names of the principal characters changed from the Greek to the Roman myths. Aphrodite became Venus, Hephaestus became known as Vulcan, and so on. Pan did not change, and Romulus, Remus, and Janus were totally Roman contributions. But despite these name changes, the basic stories and adventures remained the same.

One thing is certain, however. When Hesiod first wrote about the gods and goddesses of ancient Greece he inadvertently revealed the first "soap opera." Within the lives, loves, and hatreds of the gods lie all the stories which have provided countless plots for the literature, movies, and television shows of the modern day.

Above: The Garden of the Hesperides, wherein grew the golden apples so beloved of the goddess Hera.

Opposite: Neptune had slightly less prominence in Roman mythology than his Greek counterpart, Poseidon. But this does not detract from the magnificence of his statuary, as at the Trevi Fountain, Rome.

Chapter One
Early Greek Gods

The Creation

In the beginning there was only Chaos, a vast, dark, unformed ferment. But in Chaos existed all the elements necessary for the formation of earth and of man. Out of this ocean of tumbled forces appeared Gaea, the Mother Earth. Her first act was to divide the sea from the land, partly because she could not find any land on which to rest.

Two separate versions of the next part of the story emerge. The first recounts how Gaea, as she rested from her recent efforts, was smiled kindly upon by Chaos. He caused the rains to fall on her resting body, which created all hills and valleys, springs and watercourses, the woods and forests, and even the animals and beasts which populated the earth. The other version credits Gaea with giving birth to the Universal Egg after first being fertilized by Boreas, the North Wind. Within this egg were all the elements for creation—the moon and sun, mountains, rivers, forests, deserts, seas and oceans, and all living beings. Then Gaea gave birth to a son named Uranus.

Left: An early woodcut depicting the Great Mother. Variously identified in both Greek and Roman lore as Rhea, Gaea, Cybele, Ops, or Ceres.

Opposite: The Serpent Priestess of Crete, a priestess of the Earth Mother who predates the Greeks. The two serpents are fertility symbols.

Right: The Titans, children of Uranus and Gaea, fought against the gods for supremacy of the world. When they lost, they were banished to Tartarus, the infernal region.

Uranus

Uranus was the god of the starlit sky and heaven. He lay with his mother Gaea and from their union Gaea gave birth to many children. First came the twelve Titans, children of enormous strength and size. There were six males: Coeus, Crius, Cronus, Hyperion, Iapetus, and Oceanus; and six females: Mnemosyne, Phoebe, Rhea, Tethys, Theia, and Themis. Gaea also gave birth to the three Cyclops, each of whom had only one eye in the center of their foreheads: Arges, Brontes, and Steropes. The Cyclops were responsible for building huge walls and could provide easy fortifications. She also gave birth to three monsters: Briarius, Cottus, and Gyges. These three monsters were also known as the "hundred-handed," as each had one hundred invincible arms and fifty heads which grew from their backs. The monsters had one hundred eyes, with the capacity to keep half their eyes open while the other half could sleep, which made them ideal guardians.

Uranus was so horrified by the sight of such ugly sons and daughters that he

immediately shut them up in the underworld known as Tartarus. But this was to reckon without Gaea's feelings. She became so angry at Uranus's action that she planned not only for the release of her offspring, but for the destruction of their father Uranus.

Plotting with the Titans, and with the aid of a particularly sharp sickle which she obtained from her bosom, Gaea put forward a plan for revenge upon their father. However, none of her children were actually willing to perform such an act except for her last born son, Cronus. It was Cronus who led the rest of them into the place where Uranus was sleeping and, using the sickle, castrated his father. Immediately, all power left Uranus and Cronus was able to usurp his father's throne and rule over the earth.

According to at least one version of this tale, after unmanning Uranus, Cronus threw his genitals into the sea. They changed into white foam from which the goddess Aphrodite was born. The winds and the currents took Aphrodite first to the island of Cythera and eventually to Cyprus.

Above: A view of Lycabetus Hill from the lower slopes of the Acropolis, Athens. Lycabetus was believed to be a boulder left over from the war between the gods and the Titans.

19

Left: The Rocks of Aphrodite at Salamis, Cyprus, mark the place where Aphrodite, the Greek goddess of beauty, was born from the foam of the waves, hence her name, "Venus Anadyomere."

Right: Cronus (Saturnus, in Roman mythology) carrying a scythe and a measuring rod, with his son Zeus (identified with Jupiter, in Roman terms).

Above: The Omphalos Stone of Delphi, which the Greeks believed marked the very center of the world.

Cronus

Cronus's first act upon gaining mastery of the world was to release the remaining Titans and Cyclopes from Tartarus. It seems, however, that Cronus was guilty of a certain duplicity in this action, and his main intention had to do with his sister Rhea. After Cronus married Rhea, he promptly locked up the rest of the Titans and Cyclopes all over again.

It soon came to Cronus's notice that both his father and mother had made a rather important prophecy regarding succession. They prophesied that Cronus would be overthrown by one of his own children. Despite this, Rhea bore Cronus several children. She gave birth to Demeter, Hades, Hera, Hestia, Poseidon, and Zeus, although the actual order of birth varies depending on which history is consulted.

On the occasion of each birth, and to ensure against the prophecy coming true, Cronus swallowed each of his children. Rhea was so distressed by this that as the time came for the birth of her third child, she pleaded with her parents, Uranus and Gaea, to help her in some way. With their help Rhea was smuggled to the island of Crete where she gave birth to Zeus and then hid the child in a cave below Mount Dicte. Rhea returned to Cronus and presented to him what he took to be her third child, which was actually a large stone wrapped in baby clothes. Cronus duly consumed it and then continued creating the world.

Meanwhile, Gaea had arranged for Zeus to be brought up by two nymphs in a cave below Mount Dicte (Mount Ida in some tales). The infant was suckled by the goat Amaltheia, and when Zeus grew to manhood and prepared to return to face Cronus he gave one of the goat's horns to the nymphs. This horn was filled with desirable cornucopia and once emptied would magically and perpetually refill. With the help of Rhea, Zeus entered his father's household as a cup-bearer and gave Cronus a cup containing a particularly virulent potion. This promptly caused Cronus to spew up all of Zeus's brothers and sisters which he had consumed, as well as one large stone.

This now famous stone was taken and preserved at the Temple of Apollo in Delphi, the sacred temple at the foot of Mount Parnassus. It stood there as a symbol of the victory over Cronus and the release of the gods who became the Olympians. There are many tales which attest to the importance of Delphi. It was believed to be the center, or navel, of the earth, and in the temple was a large stone representing the actual navel, bound with a red cord signifying the umbilical cord. Cronus was thus vanquished by his children, who banished him to the outermost limits of the earth, never to return.

Left: All that remains of the Temple of Zeus in Pergamon, Turkey, are the foundations of his great altar.

Chapter Two
The Olympians

ollowing the defeat of Cronus, his children formed themselves into an exclusive hierarchy of gods and set about dividing up the world between themselves. Mount Olympus was regarded as their home and here they lived out their immortal lives, making their own rules and indulging in a social life which was the envy of mortals.

There were twelve great gods and goddesses: Zeus, Apollo, Ares, Poseidon, Hermes, and Hephaestus; Hera, Athene, Artemis, Aphrodite, Demeter, and Hestia. These twelve formed an inner, very exclusive ring of principal gods. There were also a further number of divinities: Dionysus, Dione, Leto, Selene, Helios, Themis, and Eos. These were not quite of equal importance, but none the less, they enjoyed all the pleasures, social life, and responsibilities of the inner circle.

Although Hades was a brother to Zeus and of equal stature to his other brothers and sisters, he was an infrequent visitor to Olympus. His domain was the

Opposite: A Roman interpretation of Zeus in the Villa Spada, Rome. The Roman counterpart of the Greek Zeus was Jupiter.

Left: A slightly fanciful Victorian interpretation of the assembly of the gods on Mount Olympus. Most of the depictions are instantly recognizable.

Above: Zeus, father of the gods, ruler of the sky and all its moods, brandishing his lightning bolts and drawn in a golden chariot by two eagles.

Previous pages: To understand something of the esteem and awe in which Apollo's Temple at Delphi was held so many years ago, it is best to stand within the ruins very early in the day.

Underworld which he ruled with Persephone and Hecate. In addition to the inner core of deities there was a lower rank of Olympians who danced attendance and provided many services for the main gods and goddesses. This group consisted of Hebe, Ganymede, Iris, and Nemisis; the Graces; the Muses; the Horae (Dice, Irene, and Eunomia), and the Moerae (the Fates).

Zeus

Zeus was the undoubted king of the gods, ruler of the community on Olympus, and final arbiter in any disputes. All other gods were obedient to him and anyone, god or mortal, incurring his wrath would suffer terribly. This was also true of the characters of the other gods. Those who provoked the gods would suffer, but those who worshiped and paid due homage to them would be in receipt of favors.

Zeus married his sister Hera, the eldest daughter of Rhea and Cronus, and she bore him four children: Hebe, Ilithyia, Ares, and Hephaestus. By marrying Zeus, Hera became queen of the gods. But, despite the importance of her position and her undoubted power she was not, nor ever likely to be, the sole object of his affections. Zeus was not known for his fidelity, and was responsible for, and in many instances oversaw, the process of procreation!

Before Hera, Zeus had already married Metis, goddess of Wisdom, one of the many children of the Titans, Oceanus and Tethys. But, as repeatedly happened among Greek myths, Zeus was warned that any children from his union with Metis would be stronger than he and eventually overthrow him. As his father had done before him, Zeus was not going to take any chances and when Metis duly became pregnant, Zeus consumed both mother and child. He was then struck with a severe headache. Hephaestus was sent for and, fashioning a special bronze ax for the purpose, cut open Zeus's head. Immediately Metis's child, the goddess Athene, sprang forth fully armed from his head, carrying a javelin.

Zeus had also married Themis, a daughter of Gaea and Uranus and one of the twelve Titans. Themis was the goddess of Law and Order and bore Zeus several children, all of whom had a predilection for law and moral order: Eunomia, who stood for legislation; Dike for justice; and Eirene for peace. Zeus also sired the Horae, or the Seasons, and the Moerae, the Fates. Even though she produced such worthy children, Themis was not one of the main characters upon Olympus, but she remained a constant companion and advisor to Zeus.

There were also two other "marriages" before Zeus' union with Hera. The Titaness Mnemosyne provided Zeus with nine daughters, the Muses who protected the arts and sciences: Calliope (epic poetry), Clio (history), Erato (love poetry), Euterpe (lyric poetry), Melpomene (tragedy), Polyhymnia (singing and mime), Terpsichore (dance), Thalia (comedy and poetry), and Urania (astronomy). Zeus also married Eurynome, a sea-nymph and daughter of Oceanus and Tethys, and with her had three daughters known as the Graces, who provided the world with beauty and charm.

Below: A Roman mosaic from the Sanctuary of Aphrodite, Cyprus, depicting Leda and Zeus, disguised as a swan. Yet another of Zeus's amorous conquests, Leda gave birth to Castor and Pollux, Clytemnestra and Helen from this association.

Above: The remains of the temple of Hera on the island of Samos. Although born on Samos, Hera was worshiped throughout Greece and this temple was one of the largest in the ancient world.

Hera

Hera is often described as being the first-born daughter of Cronus and Rhea, yet some accounts place her somewhat further down the line. She was born on the island of Samos, and eventually became the leading goddess on Olympus. She was considered to be the epitome of femininity and, more particularly, motherhood and maternity. She was later venerated throughout Greece and the islands, and on the island of Samos was built one of the largest temples in antiquity dedicated to her name. One of the ancient names for the island of Samos was Parthenia, meaning the Virginal One, a possible allusion to the birth of the goddess on the island.

Hera was the protectress of marriage, of married women, their children, and the home. She is reputed to have had the gift of prophecy—a gift, however, which does not seem to have extended to any prediction of Zeus's philanderous activities. She remained remarkably faithful to Zeus despite extreme treatment by him.

Hera caught the eye of Zeus but was not immediately bowled over by his charm and rejected him on several occasions. Not to be outdone, Zeus turned himself into a little bird (some say a cuckoo) and, exhibiting all the signs of distress, contrived to be found by her one day. Hera picked him up and cradled him to her. Zeus immediately resumed his original form and forced himself upon her. The natural and honorable outcome of this event was a more official marriage which was

Above: An Attic red-figured amphora from around 490 B.C. depicting Dionysus, the son of Zeus and the mortal Senele.

held on Mount Olympus. This was a very grand affair with all inhabitants of Mount Olympus taking some part in the festivities, and the wedding night is supposed to have lasted for three hundred years.

In addition to her gentler, more considerate protection of women and children, Hera was also renowned for exacting terrible vengeance upon any of Zeus's many peccadilloes. This vengeance was never directly on Zeus himself, but on those who had been the cause of his infidelity.

The mortal Semele, daughter of King Cadmus, was tricked and eventually destroyed by Hera. Zeus had been visiting Semele on a regular basis but always hid his true identity from her. Hera persuaded Semele to ask her lover to appear to her in all his true magnificence. Zeus at first refused. Semele persisted, and Zeus eventually agreed. Unfortunately, the result was entirely what Hera had predicted and hoped for, as Semele was consumed by the lightning which emanated from the sight of Zeus in all his glory, a sight that was too much for mortal eyes. But Semele was already carrying Zeus's child and he rescued the infant from the flames and hid it within his own thigh, there to remain until its birth. When the child was born it was named Dionysus.

However, just as Hera may have been in her hatred of Zeus's activities, her jealousy was constantly aroused and stories of her resulting actions are many. These frequently extended to outright destruction of an individual but did include occasional, more generalized vengeance.

Following pages: The Temple of Hera at Olympia was built around 680 B.C. and is one of the oldest Doric temples still standing in any form.

Above: Many of the characters in Greek and Roman mythology have had their names immortalized in constellations. The origin of the Milky Way is supposed to have been created from the breast milk of Hera.

One of her more satisfying moments came with the fall of Troy. She had never liked Paris after he had chosen Aphrodite in preference to her during the famous Judgment of Paris episode, and she sided very definitely with the Greeks in the Trojan War. She must have been quite happy when the Trojan race was eliminated. She could also be maliciously vindictive to those who crossed her path. She turned Antigone's hair into snakes, purely because Antigone boasted of having hair more beautiful than anyone else and she continually persecuted Io, Semele's sister for many years.

Hera bore Zeus two sons, Ares, the god of war, and Hephaestus, the god of metalwork and volcanoes; and two daughters, Hebe, the goddess of youth, and Ilithyia, the goddess of child-birth.

Poseidon

Poseidon was one of the three sons of Cronus and Rhea and brother to Hades and Zeus. Following the division of the known world after the banishment of their father Cronus, Poseidon gained total command of the oceans, seas, and (some say) earthquakes. He stood second in importance to Zeus on Mount Olympus but had few of the imposing qualities of his brother Zeus. Whether from jealousy of his brother's greater position or just a general grouchiness brought on by too much association with water, Poseidon comes across as being a grumpy old god, often quarrelsome and extremely covetous. His symbol was the trident.

Poseidon built a palace beneath the Aegean sea somewhere east of the island of

Opposite: Poseidon, god of the sea. Son of Cronus and Rhea, and brother of Zeus, Poseidon was constantly invoked by all sea travelers.

Above: The foam-flecked white horses of the sea are always credited with being Poseidon's horses, not least because Poseidon was credited (allegedly) with the invention of the horse.

Evia (Eubeoa) and planned to marry. His initial marriage efforts were not exactly crowned with success but he finally picked Amphitrite, a sea nymph living on the island of Naxos. She, however, did not pick Poseidon, and fled to the Atlas Mountains. Poseidon promptly sent a dolphin to bring her to him, however unwillingly. They were married and Amphitrite gave Poseidon three sons, Benthesicyme, Rhode, and Triton. In gratitude for the dolphin's effort he was honored with a constellation in the heavens.

Poseidon did share one characteristic trait with his more illustrious brother Zeus. Poseidon caused his wife much grief with his amorous adventures by pursuing nymphs, the occasional goddess, and various mortals. Amphitrite did not, however, wreak similar vengeance on these ladies as Hera might have done, except on one particular occasion. Poseidon loved Scylla, who was then a beautiful nymph. Amphitrite threw rare herbs into the pool where Scylla was bathing which changed the maiden into a fearsome monster which forever dwelt in the seas off Cape Messina destroying passing ships and eating the crew.

Among the offspring of Poseidon's numerous activities the most notable were Theseus, whose mother was Aethra, daughter of the king of Troezen; the frightening giant Antaeus, born by Gaea; the wild horse Arion which had the power of speech, by Demeter; and Euphemus, who possessed the gift of being able to walk on water and whose mother was Europa.

Poseidon was certainly prolific and was regarded very highly by the Greeks. As he held sway over the sea, his blessing was invoked on all voyages. He was also credited with protection over horses. He once boasted that he had actually invented the horse.

Opposite: The Tritons were half-man, half-fish. Of rather fearsome aspect and lascivious nature, they inhabited the oceans, occasionally coming ashore to create a certain amount of mischief.

36

Above: This magnificent life-size statue of Poseidon was only recovered in 1928 from the sea off Cape Artemision, north of Eubeoa.

Opposite: Eleusis, just west of Athens, was the site for some of the great "mystery" celebrations, where feasts of purification and renewal took place, often under the guidance of Demeter.

Demeter

Demeter was the goddess of the harvest, springtime, fruits, and grain. The corn-goddess was a gentle soul by nature, yet not quite as staid in her amorous endeavors as might be thought. In her early days (before marriage), she had a son, Plutus, by the Titan Iasius, who was conceived during a wedding reception they both attended. Zeus was so angry when he discovered that the Titan had lain with his sister that he killed him.

Poseidon lusted after Demeter and despite her fleeing to Attica and disguising herself as a mare, he caught up with her and she gave birth to the wild horse Arion which was gifted with speech. She also had a daughter by Zeus, after, once again, first resisting his advances. This daughter Kore, also known as Persephone, was abducted by Hades who dragged her down to his underworld kingdom. The heart-broken Demeter had no idea where this had taken place, or how to find her daughter, but wandered the whole earth anxiously looking for her. As Demeter was the goddess of all growing crops her distracted wanderings caused the usual growing seasons to be disrupted. So great was the concern about this, and the prospect of famine so imminent throughout Greece, that Zeus was called upon and eventually

Left: Niobe, the epitome of maternal sorrow. The daughter of Tantalus, she had fourteen children, but following the vengeance of Latona, she lost all of them and wept herself to death, eventually turning to stone.

intervened, and he arranged with Hades for Kore to be returned to her rightful mother.

However, there was a problem. Kore had, at Hades suggestion, eaten some pomegranate which he had knowingly offered to her—the pomegranate was food of the dead and also a symbol of the union of marriage between a man and a woman. Therefore, upon her return to her mother, she had to confess what she had done. Demeter flew into a rage and vowed that no crops should ever again grow on the earth. Zeus eventually arranged an agreement between both parties that Kore would spend three months with Hades, as Queen of the Underworld, and the remaining nine months on earth with her mother. The winter months were then spent in Tartarus and she (conveniently) returned to the earth at the beginning of spring.

Hestia

An even gentler soul than her sister Demeter, Hestia was reputedly the first of Cronus and Rhea's children, and therefore worthy of respect by her brothers and sisters. She was principally worshiped as a fire deity. She was the guardian of hearth and home (in Greek her name means "hearth") and the first morsel of any official

Opposite: A view down the (now dry) water conduit of the fountain into the rock sanctuary of Demeter in Agrigento, Sicily, one of the most perfectly preserved of the sites dedicated to the Chthonic deities.

Right: Pan was, firstly, a woodland deity—a protector of shepherds and their flocks. Although often depicted as lustful and base, Pan was worshiped throughout the ancient world and, according to some sources, was the "universal god."

meal or sacrifice was always offered to Hestia. There was always a hearth within the main hall of every town, and here her sacred fire was kept burning.

Hestia had deliberately not married and had even taken a vow of chastity on Olympus. She never encouraged amorous advances, even though both Apollo and Poseidon requested her hand. For all her worthiness and power as a goddess she remained content to administer her gifts to any needful person and any charitable cause. She never took part in any disputes or warmongering, and she eventually relinquished her seat in the inner circle of gods on Olympus in favor of the ebullient Dionysus.

Ares

The son of Zeus and Hera, Ares was the god of War. Argumentative and belligerent, Ares would, in any conflict, change sides either for gain or just devilment. He

Above: The vast acropolis at Mycenae, the home of Agamemnon, leader of the Greek expedition against Troy.

was not regarded with any great affection throughout Greece and was feared more than loved. He had a number of equally odious companions: Deimos, Phobos, Eris, Keres, and Enyo, who each stood for the unpleasant characteristics of conflict and war. Yet Ares lost more conflicts then he ever won, but this never diverted him from the sheer pleasure he got from creating havoc.

Ares maintained a long-standing hatred of his sister Athene but was beaten by her on several occasions. Heracles did not have much liking for him either and also bettered him. Ares was the cause of the first ever murder trial in history. He had killed Halirrhothius, a son of Poseidon. Ares was finally acquitted, as he claimed that he had killed Halirrhothius as he was attempting to ravish Ares's daughter Alcippe.

It was, however, Ares' long-standing affair with his sister Aphrodite that caused the greatest concern among the rest of the "family" of gods and goddesses. They all, to some degree, disliked him. None more so than Hephaestus, to whom Aphrodite was married at the time. Yet, despite being cuckolded by her, Hephaestus had suffi-

43

cient guile to turn the matter to his advantage. Instead of directly confronting the pair on terms where Ares would have had an advantage, Hephaestus used his metal-working skills in making a gossamer thin, but incredibly strong, net. This net fell on the lovers when they were engaged with one another one evening. Hephaestus then summoned all the other gods to witness the predicament of the trapped couple. They all duly arrived and burst out laughing at the comical pairs predicament. In return for releasing the couple, Hephaestus banished Aphrodite to Cyprus and Ares to Thrace.

From their affair, Aphrodite had had three children—Harmonia, Phobus, and Deimus, whom she had previously passed off as Hephaestus's progeny. The other children whom Ares sired over the years did not fare particularly well and their lives often ended in tragedy. Cycnus, son of Pyrene, was killed by Heracles; and Phlegyas, son of Chryse, was killed by Apollo.

Hephaestus

Hephaestus was the exception when assuming that all the gods and goddesses were of wonderful looks and ideal proportioning. Hephaestus was ugly and lame from birth, but he was a skilled smith and could turn his hand to anything made in metal.

Below: The grove on the island of Cyprus where Aphrodite reputedly bathed shortly before her marriage.

Above: A depiction of the goddess Athene receiving Pandora, the mortal fashioned by Hephaestus at Zeus's command.

There is some doubt regarding his birth. He is often simply mentioned as being one of the children of Zeus and Hera, but there are also tales that Hera bore him unaided, or possibly with the "assistance" of the dwarf Cedalion. This tale is given an even greater credence, as Hera later arranged for Cedalion to teach her son the arts of metal-working. It is believed that Cedalion remained Hephaestus's constant companion wherever he traveled. Hephaestus was lame from birth and Hera was so horrified by his ugliness that she threw him from Mount Olympus and he landed in the sea. Although gravely injured, he was looked after by the seagoddess Thetis and Eurynome for nine years. During this time he developed his skills and made beautiful and clever objects in metal.

Hephaestus eventually made a golden throne and, in a well-planned revenge, sent it to his mother Hera as a gift. It naturally delighted Hera and all the gods. She promptly sat on the throne and could not move. She was struck immovable until Hephaestus was summoned to reveal the secret of the mechanism. In return for releasing his mother, Hephaestus was re-admitted to the society of the gods and married Aphrodite.

However, in a later dispute with Zeus over his treatment of his mother, Zeus threw him from Olympus again. He took all day to fall and eventually crashed on to the island of Lemnos, more dead than alive. He was cared for on the island and remained there until the Olympians realized his valuable skills and begged him to return.

Hephaestus is also linked with volcanoes, as these are believed to be the locations of his metal forges, where he worked with the faithful Cedalion.

Apollo

Famed for his good looks, Apollo, the son of Zeus and Leto, was the god associated with medicine and music. He was also the god of reason, light, truth, and prophecy, and a natural manager of the shrine at Delphi. He was also regarded as the sun-god, but this probably refers more to the "light of reason and truth" than to his being a personification of the sun. The sun was in the sole keeping of Helios, son of Hyperion and Thea, who drove his magnificent chariot across the sky each day.

Apollo's mother, Leto, daughter of the Titans Coeus and Phoebe, was one of Zeus's many lovers and, consequently, received the full force of Hera's jealous

wrath. Shortly before the impending birth of Leto's twins, Hera had demanded that Leto should be turned away from anywhere it was possible to complete her confinement. She had further prophesied that the child would only be born "where the sun did not shine." Every country turned Leto away and she wandered Greece desperately searching for sanctuary, and constantly harried by the serpent Python. She was eventually carried by the wind, or a dolphin, to the floating island of Ortygia in the center of the Aegean. When the time came for the actual birth, Poseidon, who probably had no love for Hera, created a vast wave to cover the island at the moment of the children's birth. Apollo and Artemis were then born on the island, which later became known as Delos, a sacred island.

Apollo's love life was somewhat varied, and while he was undoubtedly endowed with grace, beauty, charm, and strength, at times his adventures were distinctly tragic. He loved both men and women, but with the emphasis firmly on the latter. His particular penchant seems to have been for mortal women and nymphs.

On one occasion he was pursuing a nymph called Daphne. She managed to elude him several times but Apollo finally caught her and all seemed lost. But Daphne

Opposite: Virtually all that remains of the magnificent ancient city of Corinth are these few columns of the Temple of Apollo. Earthquakes and belligerent Romans are responsible for the rest.

Following pages: The sacred island of Delos, at the center of the Cyclades, was the birthplace of Apollo and Artemis.

Left: Artemis (the Roman goddess Diana) was regarded as the moon goddess, but was more frequently associated with hunting and woodlands.

cried out to Gaea for help and was immediately transformed into a laurel tree.

A more tragic tale relates how Coronis, daughter of Phlegyas, became pregnant with Apollo's child, but just before the birth was due she married Ischys. Apollo had previously left a crow to watch over her while he was away. This crow immediately flew to Apollo telling him of the marriage. Apollo was so angry that he caused the deaths of both Coronis and her new husband and also turned the crow's feathers to deepest black. It was fortunate, however, that Apollo arrived at the twin funerals of Coronis and Ischthys for, as the bodies were being consumed by fire, Apollo retrieved the unborn child. This child was Asclepius, the god of medicine.

The tale of Apollo and Hyacinthus is the most well-known within those of Apollo's male-orientated loves. The handsome Hyacinthus was loved not only by Apollo but by several others as well. One of these, Zephyrus the West Wind, came upon Apollo teaching Hyacinthus how to throw the discus. In a jealous rage Zephyrus diverted the course of the discus, causing it to strike Hyacinthus on the head, killing him. Tradition has it that from the drops of his blood the hyacinth flower grew.

Opposite: Apollo finally slew the Python within the confines of the sacred temple at Delphi. Despite Zeus's anger, later worshipers of Apollo enlarged the temple.

Above: The naiads were the nymphs of the watercourses, brooks, rivers, and streams. They were benevolent beings who were often gifted with the power of prophecy.

There was also a certain vicious streak in Apollo's character, and he was not averse to bringing down a terrible vengeance upon both deities and mortals. After killing the satyr Marsyas following a flute playing contest, Apollo flayed him alive and fixed the satyr's skin to a pine tree. He slew the giant Tityus for making advances on his mother Leto, by spread-eagling him on the ground so that his liver was devoured by vultures.

Although Apollo was highly regarded among the gods of Olympus, he managed to incur the wrath of Zeus on several occasions. Very early in his life he had pursued the serpent Python (which had, at Hera's command, pursued Apollo's mother Leto before his birth) and he foolishly entered the sacred temple at Delphi and slew the Python within the main temple area. This incurred the anger of Zeus, who banished him to Tempe, a steep wooded valley between Mount Olympus and Mount Ossa. Apollo, ever the querulous offspring, totally ignored this command and went somewhere else instead.

Apollo was good-looking and gifted, but his personality did not always match his physical characteristics.

Artemis

The twin sister of Apollo, Artemis is often referred to as the Virgin Huntress. She shared much of Apollo's early life after their birth on the isle of Delos, learning the same skills and even accompanying him when he slew the serpent Python at Delphi. She was very much a mythological equivalent of today's tomboy. She preferred hunting and the thrill of the chase and she shared Apollo's gift for archery. Even at an early age, when asked by her father for anything which he could grant her, she asked for a bow to match that of her brother's. In addition, she also requested eternal virginity.

She finally parted company from Apollo and settled instead in Arcadia, spending all her time hunting with a pack of hounds given to her by Pan, and accompanied by sixty sea-nymphs and twenty river nymphs. Artemis refused all advances from men and further demanded the same chaste character from her constant companions as she maintained for herself.

That same rather vindictive streak which was evident in Apollo was also present in Artemis's character. If ever she was slighted, or even annoyed by someone else, she was capable of wreaking terrible vengeance upon them.

Left: Eros, the mischievous god of love. Of doubtful parentage, he was the faithful attendant of Aphrodite, but prey to the same emotions he induced in others.

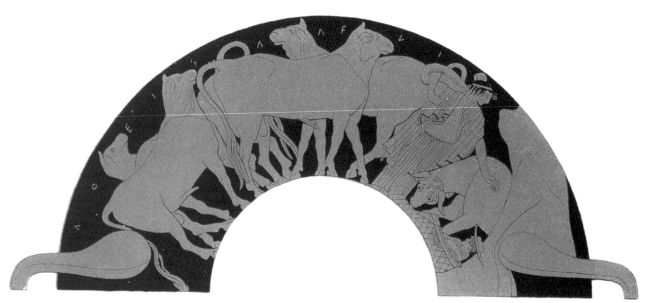

was the daughter of Oceanus and Tethys and a rather insignificant deity and one of the "outer" ring of Olympian characters.

The first version of the goddess's birth proved far more popular, as it struck the right notes of drama, mystery, and excitement. Aphrodite was always considered a creature of the greatest beauty and far more overtly seductive than her counterparts on Olympia. In order to finally test which of the three goddesses—Hera, Artemis, and Aphrodite—was the most beautiful, a contest was devised. Paris, the handsome son of King Priam of Troy, was appointed the judge and each of the three women appeared to him in turn. Each promised much that the embarrassed youth might desire. In the end he chose the seductive charms of Aphrodite. In return Aphrodite granted Paris the affections of Helen, wife of Menaleus, an act which was to directly cause the Trojan War.

Although well gifted with sexual charm and a certain amount of infidelity along the way, Aphrodite was also venerated as the protectress of marriage and unions and she continued to spread "life giving joy wherever she went." However, her actions occasionally angered Zeus, so much so that on one occasion he created in her a desire for a mortal man rather than one of the Immortals. The shepherd Anchises then became the object of her desire. She appeared to him disguised as a mortal as he was tending his flocks, made love to him, and only in the morning revealed to him who she was. He was naturally terrified and feared for his life. Aphrodite calmed his fears if he promised not to reveal to the child the true identi-

Above: The god of wine, jollity, and much orgiastic enjoyment, Dionysus was first depicted as an old man with a jolly countenance.

Opposite, above: Greek red-figure work vase depicting Apollo reclaiming his cattle from the infant Hermes.

Opposite, below: In addition to the "Olympic" games performed at Olympia and Corinth, Delphi also staged athletic tournaments, at which the statue or effigy of Mercury would be displayed.

Above: The Ear of Dionysus, a natural cave at Syracuse, in Sicily.

ty of its mother. The child was Aeneas, who became one of the Heroes.

Aphrodite also used her sexual wiles on members of the Olympian fraternity. Most notably, she presented three children to Ares: Pheobus, Deimus, and Harmonia. She also managed to spend time with Hermes, the outcome of their union being Hermaphroditus; Poseidon, to whom she presented two sons, Herophilus and Rhodis; and Dionysus. The offspring of this meeting being Priapus, a rather ugly youth endowed with unusually large genitalia.

The other great, but tragic love of Aphrodite's life was Adonis. He was a beautiful youth who had been born when Smyrna, daughter of King Cyniras of Cyprus had been changed into a myrtle tree. Aphrodite found the child and gave him to Persephone for safe keeping. Years after, Aphrodite returned to reclaim the infant. Persephone refused to give him up as the child had now grown into a youth of great beauty. Aphrodite appealed to Zeus, who came up with the compromise that Adonis should spend one third of the year with Persephone, another third with Aphrodite, and the final third on his own. This was agreed, but Aphrodite cheated. She used her magic girdle to capture Adonis's heart for that period of the year allowed to himself. This not only angered Persephone but also came to Ares's knowledge. Jealous of Adonis, Ares took on the form of a wild boar which attacked and killed Adonis. Aphrodite found the dying Adonis and it is said that from his blood the gentle anemone flower grew, and from Aphrodite's tears a white rose emerged.

The Pleiades

The daughters of Atlas and Pleione, the Pleiades were Maia, Taygete, Electra, Alcyone, Celoeno, Sterope, and Merope. All seven were being pursued by Orion and, in order to save them, Zeus turned them into doves and eventually into stars.

All the sisters except Merope were loved by the gods, but Merope's star is the faintest of those in the constellation of the Pleiades. Gentle and beneficent beings, their constellation appeared in the Greek sky just before the start of the warmer weather in May.

Hermes

The messenger and the herald of the gods, Hermes was the son of Zeus from his out-of-wedlock liaison with Maia, daughter of Atlas. In addition to his regular duties carrying messages to and from Zeus, between the other gods and mortals, he was also the god associated with communications and, in particular, communicators—writers, orators, and even travelers. He was also the protector of mischief-makers and rascals, which particularly suited his often devious character. His underhandedness was well-known, yet it was said that he never told a lie.

Hermes's deviousness started very early in his life. On the day that he was born he left his cradle in the morning and before noon killed a tortoise, fitted the shell with strings, and made a beautiful sounding lyre. He then proceeded to steal fifty

Above: Centaurs had the head, torso, and arms of a man and the lower half of a horse. Part of Dionysus's company of merrymakers, they were often regarded as drunken and licentious.

Following pages: The Temple of Apollo at Didyma in Turkey was designed by the Greek architects Paeorios of Ephesos and Daphnis of Miletus. It was started in 313 B.C. and finished around 40 B.C.

61

cattle from Apollo, making them all walk backwards so that they could not easily be traced. He then resumed his place in his cradle. Unfortunately, he had been seen stealing the cattle by a man working in a nearby field who promptly told Apollo. Hermes managed to calm Apollo by giving him the lyre which he had made earlier. So entranced was Apollo with the gift that he repaid Hermes with the original fifty cattle and bestowed other powers on the child.

In the earliest days of veneration Hermes was regarded as the protector of herds and shepherds. They would often place an image of Hermes above the doors of their dwellings. Being the protector of travelers as well, this imagery could also be seen at the junctions of roads in the countryside and at street corners in towns and cities.

Hermes wore winged-shoes, or sandals, a round helmet-shaped hat, and carried a staff entwined with serpents (a symbol which later was adopted by the medical profession). Because of his speed and agility he became a favorite god of athletes and his effigy was placed in a prominent position at athletic meetings.

Hermes had a mind which was not only devious but very clever, and he was very inquisitive. He helped in the construction of the alphabet and invented games, the science of astronomy, and the musical scale. He also assisted Hades in guiding dying souls gently to the underworld by acting as their traveling companion.

Dionysus

Son of Zeus and the mortal Semele, Dionysus is most notable for providing the world with the gift of wine, and he became synonymous with revelry, merriment, orgies, and the sheer joy of life.

Dionysus's birth was not very auspicious. Because of Hera's jealousy of Zeus's attentions upon Semele, she firstly tricked Dionysus's mother Semele into requesting Zeus to appear to her in his full glory—she was fatally burned by the experience—and then later arranging for the Titans to abduct the newborn child and tear him to pieces. Zeus rescued Dionysus from being consumed by fire on the first occasion by hiding the unborn child in his own thigh until he was born. Rhea, his grandmother, managed to thwart the second attempt on his life and gave Dionysus to Ino, Semele's sister and the wife of King Athamas, to care for. However Hera's vengeance struck yet again as she drove both Ino and her husband mad. Dionysus was then disguised as a goat, spending the remainder of his childhood being brought up by the nymphs of Nysa. Although considerable doubt is placed on the actual location of Nysa, the island of Naxos has a very strong claim upon it. It was while he lived with the nymphs on the island that he invented wine, which was to prove his greatest gift to the world.

Dionysus was also famous for his travels and adventures. These were not only confined to the known world of Greece and the islands but extended far beyond the eastern boarders, through Syria, and as far as India. In all his wanderings he carried with him the evidence and the knowledge of the vine, its cultivation and winemaking. On his return to Greece, his new found confidence and the altered appearance which he displayed did not sit well. He was constantly mistaken for a lesser personage and often slighted by those he visited. Until, that is, the demonstrations of his powers (only gods had the power to change people into other forms) forced people to acknowledge that the screech owl, the mouse, and the owl were indeed their own children who had unwisely refused to join in Dionysus's festivities and ceremonies.

For the gift of the vine and because his father was a god, Dionysus was later accepted as one of the twelve gods of Olympus. A place was provided for him following Hestia's decision to leave Olympus.

Above: Hera, the wife of Zeus, was the protectress of marriage, married women, children, and the home. She was faithful to Zeus despite his many peccadilloes.

Opposite: Athene was the protectress of Athens and many other cities in Greece, but her finest temple was within the Parthenon on the Acropolis.

Above: The unforgettable temple of Aphaeia on the island of Aegina, first ascribed to the cult of Athene. Aphaeia was the daughter of Zeus and Carme.

Athene

Athene was Zeus's favorite daughter. The nature of her birth was distinctly unusual. Zeus had pursued the Titaness Metis and had seduced her, despite her protestations. Metis became pregnant with Zeus's child. Gaea appeared to Zeus and told him that, although the expected child was a girl, if Metis should ever produce a son it would be mightier than Zeus and would overthrow him. Zeus promptly disposed of Metis by eating her.

A little while after, Zeus was overcome by a very violent headache. With the assistance of Hermes (in some tales it was Hephaestus), they split open Zeus's skull and out sprang Athene fully dressed for battle. She became a charming and very protective goddess. Her chief protection was reserved for the arts and crafts, learning, the intellect and women's arts, and the city of Athens. Although she was born as a warrior goddess, Athene was particularly concerned with the actual justice of war, and was a strong champion of the brave and honorable. She never lost in battle and was a great strategist. She was also protectress of all those whose causes she deemed to be just.

With her gifts for arts and crafts she introduced weaving and embroidery, invented the potters wheel, and assisted in the design and building of Jason's ship the Argo. Athene was undoubtedly proud of her abilities and refused to be outdone by others. A certain maiden Arachne, living in the eastern kingdom of Lydia, had boasted of her supreme prowess as an embroiderer. Athene disguised herself as an old woman and challenged Arachne to a contest. Arachne's work was so perfect and of such amazing quality that Athene couldn't find any flaw in it. Incensed by her failure to find fault in Arachne's work, Athene changed Arachne into a spider and condemned her to perpetually weave patterns with the thread from her own body.

Being Zeus's favorite daughter brought with it a certain amount of envy from the rest of the Olympians. But despite this, Athene had no shortage of suitors. She resisted all advances and remained chaste, yet this did not stop certain individuals from trying to win her affections. The only one who came close to forming a union with Athene was her brother Hephaestus. On one occasion, when he was making a set of arms for her, and when all his previous declarations of love had been ignored, he attempted to ravish her. She escaped just in time and Hephaestus's seed fell harmlessly on the ground. The seed fertilized and gave birth to a boy, Erichthonius.

Athene later found the child and raised him as though he were her own. She did, however, managed to keep the child secret from the other gods which spared her the embarrassment of explaining the circumstances of its birth. Erichthonius later became king of Athens and dedicated temples to Athene in the city.

Athene's symbol was the owl and she gave the world the olive tree. She was protectress of several cites in Greece, in addition to Athens.

Left: Athene was born, fully clad for battle, emerging from the head of Zeus to become his trusted daughter.

Chapter Three

Attendant Gods

Helios, the God of the Sun

Helios was the son of the Titans Hyperion and Thea and his sisters were Selene, the goddess of the Moon, and Eos, the Dawn. Between them, they took care of both the day and the night. It was Helios's duty to rise at the first cock crow and then to ride his magnificent chariot across the sky westwards until he reached the farthest point of the known world, the Isles of the Blessed. There he descended into the surrounding sea and was carried back to the east to begin his daily journey all over again the following morning.

The Greeks believed the earth was flat and the land was surrounded by a great circle of water. They witnessed every day and night that the sun, the moon, and all the stars always appeared in the same area of the sky, crossed the great domed heaven above them, and then vanished. Hence their belief that all these things were carried back to their starting point by the great surrounding ocean stream. A further indication of the way in which the Greeks viewed the world comes when we find that Helios's home was in the island of Rhodes, which the Greeks considered to be one of the furthest points east.

Opposite: The "Ferryman of the Dead," Charon took the spirits of the dead across the River Styx to Hades. It was traditional to place a coin in the mouth of the dead as a toll for the ferryman.

Left: The goddess Eos (Roman equivalent Aurora) was the herald of the dawn. She announced the new day and then traveled with her brother Helios across the daytime sky.

Hic canet errantē Lunam, Solisq; labores
Arčturūq;,pluuiasq; hyad.gēinosq; triōes

The island of Rhodes became Helios's home by an incident which shows something of his character. Helios was an exception to the trait which was very evident among the gods and goddesses—that of jealousy and anger often induced by someone else gaining an advantage. When Zeus was dividing up the world and allotting tasks and domains to each of the Olympians he forgot poor Helios. When he realized his mistake, and was about to start the task all over again, Helios gently pointed out that it was all very simple, as he did not mind, and he had just spotted an island which was emerging far in the eastern sea and which looked ideal for his purposes. Zeus gratefully gave it to him.

Helios was married to a nymph, Rhode, the daughter of Poseidon, and she bore him eight children. He named his new island home in honor of her. Three of Helios's grandchildren have given their names to towns on the island of Rhodes.

He was an all-seeing god as he had the ability to look down from on high and watch everything beneath him. It was Helios who told Hephaestus about Aphrodite's liaisons with Ares. Aphrodite's response to this was to cause Helios to fall in love with a considerable number of goddesses and mortal women. As a consequence he fathered many children, two who were of special interest.

Helios's son Phaethon needed confirmation of his divine birth to settle an argument. Helios granted his son anything he asked in order to prove the point to others. Phaethon settled for being able to ride his father's chariot across the sky. Helios was forced to reluctantly agree, but Phaethon's inexperience caused his demise. The sheer excitement of driving this magnificent chariot was fine to begin with, but as soon as the horses realized the inexperience of their new driver they took advantage of it. They charged about the sky completely out of control. They came too near the earth and burned up vast tracts of land and dried up all the rivers. Zeus finally lost his temper and destroyed both the chariot and young Phaethon. It is believed that Phaethon was responsible for the deserts of Africa.

Helios also had a daughter called Circe. She lived on the island of Aeaea and cast a spell over the whole island. This spell caused all who landed there to be turned into various forms of animals. All Odysseus's crew were caught in this way and only released after Odysseus had spent one year of forgetfulness on the island with Circe. The only reason Odysseus was not affected in the same manner as his crew was because he was been able to ward off the effects with the magic herb moly, given to him by Hermes.

Below: The Necromanteion at Ephyra in northern Greece was a shrine where both Greeks and Romans tried to raise the spirits of the dead in order that they might learn of the future.

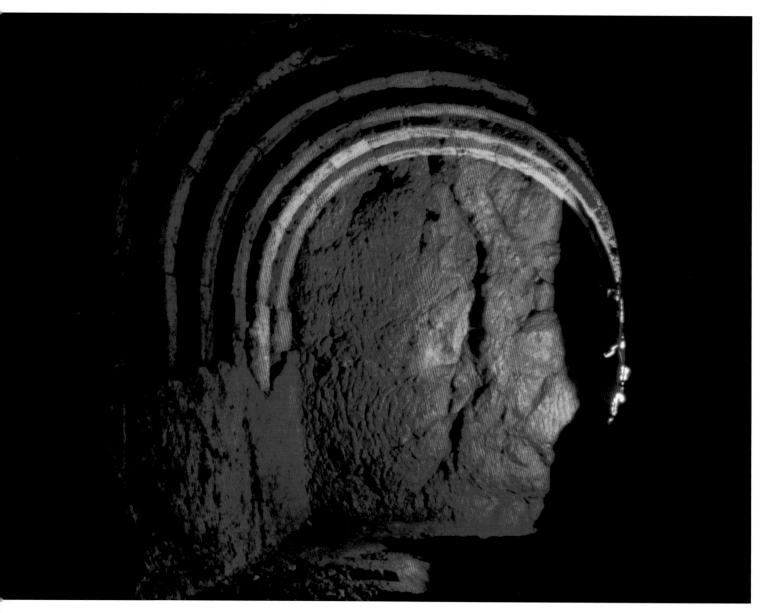

Selene, Goddess of the Moon

When her brother Helios had completed his ride across the sky each day, Selene's work began. Clad in magnificent white robes and riding in a chariot drawn by brightly shining horses, she traversed the night sky watching over the sleep of all mortals. There are always two versions of the famous tale of Selene and Endymion. In the first, Selene was captivated by the beauty of the shepherd son's as she crossed the sky. She placed on him the spell of perpetual sleep just so that she could visit him each night and kiss his cheek. The other version relates how Selene had fifty children by Endymion but then he was cursed with eternal sleep by Zeus for having made advances towards Hera.

Eos, the Winged Goddess of the Dawn

Eos, the daughter of Hyperion, and sister of Selene and Helios, rose each day before Helios in order to announce the imminent arrival of the sun. She then accompanied her brother as he rode the daytime sky. She, like her brother, also fell foul of Aphrodite's vengeful nature. But whereas this had happened because her brother had told tales of Aphrodite's infidelity, Eos had been discovered in Ares's

Following pages: Lake Stymphalos, where Heracles, the son of Zeus and Alcmena, fought the iron-winged and iron-beaked Stymphalian Birds as one of his Twelve Labors.

73

bed. Aphrodite's curse was an intriguing one. For the rest of eternity, Eos would repeatedly fall in love with a succession of young mortals.

Within this stream of many young men, Eos fell in love with Tithonus and married him. She also deeply wished for Tithonus to be granted eternal life so that she could remain with him for eternity. She approached Zeus and was successful in her request. Unfortunately, while asking for and receiving the gift of immortality for her lover, she omitted to ask that he should remain forever young! As the years went by, Tithonus became older and older and increasingly decrepit. He became a mere shell of a body with a high-pitched grating voice. The gods finally took pity on him and transformed him into a cicada.

Themis

A Titaness, Themis was the daughter of Uranus and Gaia and a goddess personifying justice. She was also one of a number of "lesser gods" just slightly removed from the inner circle of important deities on Olympus. Themis had been married to Zeus even before his marriage to Hera. But that does not have appeared to have brought down upon her the customary curses of Hera. In fact, Themis remained on hand to advise Zeus with Hera's full consent. Themis had a marvelous ability for stage managing the assemblies on Olympus. She summoned the gods together, kept order over the proceedings, and frequently offered good advice.

As befitted one who was the goddess of justice, she gave birth to similarly inclined children. The Horae were three sisters: Eunomia, who stood for good order; Dice, justice; and Irene, peace. She also bore the Fates (the Moerae), three dispassionate beings who controlled the lives of all men. Atropos, the first-born and the one who severs the thread of life; Clotho, who watched over birth and spun the thread of life; and Lachesis, the one who decided the length of the thread of life.

Hebe

Hebe was the provider of youth and vitality and the cup bearer to the gods. She helped Themis by performing general duties at the assemblies of the gods. Her prime role was to carry the nectar and ambrosia around, refilling any vessels when required. She also undertook general duties for various gods and is often regarded as a young, beautiful domestic for the company. She lost her position at one stage and for some slight indiscretion, and was replaced by Ganymede. However, and as something of a consolation, she was granted the hand of Heracles when he ascended to Olympus and achieved the status of a god.

Iris, Goddess of the Rainbow

Iris was the goddess of the rainbow and married to Zephyrus, the West Wind. In her capacity as a messenger of the gods, and of Zeus's communications in particular, Iris traveled down the stairway of the rainbow from heaven to earth. Like her counterparts Hebe and Themis, she had her duties among the company of gods helping to unhitch chariots, running baths, and supplying nectar. Iris was particularly devoted to Hera for whom she acted in much the manner of a general servant. She also delivered all Hera's messages, and even carried out some of her vengeful acts.

Ganymede

A Trojan youth, Ganymede took over Hebe's cup-bearing duties on Olympus. Zeus had spotted the handsome youth and decided that such an asset should be introduced to Olympian company, despite the youth not being of divine birth. Taking the form of an eagle, Zeus flew down and picked Ganymede up, then flew back to Olympus and installed him as his own cup-bearer.

Opposite: The awesome sacred temple of Delphi at the foot of Mount Parnassus is regarded as the "navel of the earth" and seat of the celebrated Oracle.

Chapter Four

The Heroes

Heracles

The greatest athlete and of superhuman strength, Heracles was the son of Zeus and Alcmena, daughter of Electryon, King of Mycenae. Alcmena was yet another of the many mortals with whom Zeus dallied. One of the most popular tales relates how Zeus disguised himself as Alcmena's husband, Amphitryon. Choosing his moment carefully to coincide with the absence of her husband, Zeus so altered the aspect of time that he managed to lie with Alcmena for the equivalent of three whole nights, but to all outside observers it appeared that just a few hours had passed.

Alcmena's real husband Amphitryon returned home soon after Zeus's exploits, totally unaware of what had happened. He also made love to Alcmena and soon after she became pregnant with twin boys: Heracles, the son of Zeus, and Iphicles, the son of Amphitryon. Zeus was always anxious to sire a son who could defend and protect both mortals and Immortals. In this respect Heracles was a very worthy son.

It wasn't long, however, before Hera appeared upon the scene. Hearing that Zeus had made an oath that a descendant of Perseus would one day rule Greece, she realized to her consternation that Alcmena was a granddaughter of Perseus. Angered at yet another dalliance by her husband Zeus, she tried to ensure that Zeus's prophecy did not come true. Hera sent two serpents to attack the infants Heracles and Iphicles. But while Iphicles cried out in terror, Heracles dispatched both serpents with his bare hands. Fearing more attacks from Hera, both infants were then given into the tender care of shepherds. Heracles spent all his childhood developing his natural gifts of strength and stamina.

In his later youth Heracles killed a lion which had been threatening his adopted

Opposite: The Eumenides, whose name means "Kindly Ones," were also known as the Furies or the Dogs of Hades. They wreaked vengeance on anyone committing patricide, but were worshiped throughout Greece for their more benevolent qualities.

Below: A marriage scene, possibly depicting Heracles' union with Megara, with Artemis and Apollo attending the festivities.

Left: Heracles' final task was to return with the fearsome three-headed dog Cerberus from the Underworld. Having performed the task, and his Labors, Heracles let the dog return to Hades to guard the gates.

Left: Ares' gift to Hippolyte, the queen of the Amazons, was a magic girdle that Heracles managed to acquire in the course of his Twelve Labors.

father's herds. He not only performed this act with great skill but, in very much the same manner as his father Zeus might have done, whiled away the time waiting for the lion by sleeping with fifty young women. Hera never gave up in her attempts against him and bided her time.

The Labors of Heracles

Heracles had been given the hand of Megara, daughter of King Creon, for his help in defeating Creon's enemies. This proved to be the moment for Hera to strike and she set the Fury of Madness on him. This madness had tragic results for Heracles. Believing that his children and his wife Megara were his worst enemies, he killed all of them. For this dreadful crime the Oracle at Delphi decreed that he could

Opposite: The first of Heracles' Labors was to dispatch the Nemean Lion, which he wrestled to death and then used the skin for his own protection. From a fourth-century vase.

Above: The architectural genius of the palaces of Knossos, Crete. They were the setting for the tale of Theseus and his triumph over the Minotaur.

only remove the shame and guilt by going to Eurystheus and undertaking any tasks he set for him during the next twelve years.

The Nemean Lion

Heracles was commanded to kill the Nemean Lion which had been destroying the Nemean countryside, killing and devouring anything it came across. It was impossible to penetrate its skin with arrows, sword, or spear. Heracles finally tracked the lion to its lair and soon realized how invulnerable it was. The only recourse was for Heracles to face it unarmed. He trapped it in its cave and wrestled with it, eventually strangling the beast. He returned to Eurystheus with his prize and used the invulnerable skin of the lion for his own future protection.

82

The Lernaean Hydra

Following his success against the Nemean Lion, Heracles's next allotted task was to kill a terrifying monster in the swamps of Lerna in the Peloponnese. The serpent had many heads, each breathing fumes which were fatal. When a head was cut off, another would grow in its place. Hera had concocted this terrible beast and also sent a vicious crab to add to Heracles's troubles. He eventually slew the beast with the help of Iolaus, son of Iphicles. He seared the stumps of each neck with burning brands and dipped his arrows in the poisonous blood making the wounds fatal. Heracles buried the one immortal head of the Hydra under a rock.

The Erymanthian Boar

The Erymanthian Boar lived in Arcadia, devastating the countryside. As he had to catch the beast alive, Heracles pursued it until it was exhausted and then carried it back to Eurystheus.

The Stymphalian Birds

The wings and beaks of the Stymphalian Birds were of iron and they had total command of the countryside around Lake Stymphalus. After first frightening them by smashing cymbals together and dispersing them, Heracles slew most of them with his arrows and drove the rest away.

The Hind of Ceryneia

Heracles spent a whole year tracking and finally overcoming the hind which had hooves of bronze and golden horns.

The Cretan Bull

A gift from Poseidon to King Minos of Crete, this gigantic black bull had gone mad and created havoc in the area. Heracles captured it alive and (as some report) rode it back to Mycenae. Having then released the bull, it settled near Marathon, only to be killed later by Theseus.

The Girdle of the Amazons

Eurystheus's daughter Admete desired the magic girdle which Hippolyte, the Queen of the Amazons, had been given by Ares. Heracles traveled to Cappadocia with other heroes, including Theseus and Telamon, and obtained the girdle quite easily from the Amazon Queen. Hera was incensed at this success and spread a rumor among the Amazons that the visitors were planning to abduct the queen. Open war broke out in which the heroes were victorious.

The Augean Stables

Augeas, king of Elis, kept an enormous herd of cattle. Hercules's task was to clear up the stables in just one day. So great was the accumulation of waste that the task appeared impossible. Heracles diverted the river Alpheus through the yard and completed the task.

Above: The Lerna marshes, where Heracles battled with and overcame the many-headed Hydra.

Opposite: It is supposed that King Aegeus was standing at the temple of Poseidon on Cape Sounion, watching for the return of his son Theseus from fighting the Minotaur, when he assumed his son was dead and threw himself into the sea in his grief.

The Horses of Diomedes

The horses belonged to Diomedes, a son of Ares, who ruled in Thrace. These wild animals had been fed continuously on human flesh. When Heracles arrived with his companions, they first killed Diomedes and his attendants and then fed their remains to the horses. The horses instantly became tame and were led back to Mycenae.

The Oxen of Geryon

For this task Heracles traveled far to the west to the kingdom of Iberia where Geryon kept his famous beasts. Heracles slew Geryon, his dog Orthrus, and the herdsman Eurytion. In praise of his victory Heracles set up the pillars which still bear his name. The harder part of the task was to bring the cattle back to Greece. On the way Heracles had to kill two sons of Poseidon who tried to steal the cattle; he had to fight Eryx in Sicily, after one of the oxen had been secreted away by him; and even when he got to Greece, Hera sent a gadfly which drove the beasts wild and dispersed them all over the countryside. Heracles eventually rounded them all up and returned to Mycenae. Eurystheus promptly sacrificed all the cattle to Hera.

Above: The three-headed dog Cerberus, guardian of the Underworld.

The Golden Apples of the Hesperides

The task was to return with the famous golden apples, but first Heracles had to find out how to get to the Hesperides. On advice, he was told to consult the elusive Nereus, the father of the Nereids and the original "Old Man of the Sea." Heracles finally captured Nereus and forced him to reveal how to reach the Hesperides.

Along the way, Heracles defeated pygmies; wrestled with Antaeus, who regained strength as long as his feet touched the ground but Heracles defeated him by holding him high up in the air until he expired; he killed the eagle which fed off the liver of Prometheus; and, after many other adventures finally obtained the Golden Apples. When he presented the apples to Eurystheus he gave them back to Heracles. He, in turn gave them to Athene, who returned them to the Hesperides.

The Final Task

Heracles's final task, now that Eurystheus was despairing of ever defeating Heracles, was to bring back Cerberus from the Underworld. Heracles ventured into the Underworld and succeeded in wounding Hades and was able to overcome Cerberus with his bare hands. On returning to Mycenae, Eurystheus released Heracles from his labors.

Heracles did not retire gracefully after all these efforts, but instead headed out on further adventures. These were numerous, invariably involving the death and destruction of any enemies Heracles had encountered. Finally he decided to return to punish Eurystheus and claim the hand of the king's whose daughter had been promised to him. He duly killed Eurytus and his sons and made off with his daughter, Iole. However, as he put on a cloak soaked with the blood of the centaur who had previously been killed, Heracles was fatally consumed by fire. Just before he perished, Zeus rescued him, bringing him to Olympus and installing him with the Immortals.

dragon's teeth which Jason had brought with him as a gift from Athene. It was well-known that these teeth would rise up as fully-armed warriors and fight against the sower.

Aeetes' daughter, Medea, had fallen in love with Jason when he arrived and, with her help, he completed the tasks. She first helped him to yoke the bulls and provided him with a magical lotion which warded off any harmful effects of the beasts. He plowed the field as required and sowed the dragon's teeth. The moment the armed warriors appeared he cleverly turned them against each other and slew any that remained.

But Aeetes had no intention of releasing the fleece and threatened to kill all the Argonauts and burn the ship. Medea, fortunately, had overheard Aeetes' plans for this and conveyed the news to Jason. At dead of night she took them secretly to the sacred grove of Ares where the fleece hung. Using a special distillation of herbs she soothed the dragon and, while it slept, Jason was able to retrieve the Golden Fleece.

Jason and his Argonauts had many more adventures before finally returning to Greece. Jason and Medea married and remained together for several years. Finally Jason grew tired of her and married another. Medea was overcome with rage and presented a beautiful gown to the new bride which, when she put it on, totally consumed her in fire. Medea then killed all the children she had bore with Jason and fled to Athens. It is told that Jason eventually grew tired, not only of his new wife but of life in general, and died of melancholy. One other version has it that he was asleep under the prow of the Argo when it fell down and killed him.

Perseus

Perseus was the son of Zeus and Danae. She was the only child of King Agrisius who was desperate for a son. But when he consulted the Oracle of Delphi he was informed that he would have no son, but that his grandson would destroy him. He duly took the precaution of incarcerating his daughter far from the influence of any man. However, Zeus appeared to her and gave her a child. Agrisius shut up both mother and child in a cask and cast them into the sea. They were saved by the intervention of Zeus and came to rest on the island of Seriphos.

Perseus is remembered most for his attempt to bring back the Gorgon Medusa's head. He was aided in his efforts by Athene. She told him that he must never look directly at the head or he would be turned to stone. There were other things that Perseus needed including winged sandals, a magic bag to contain the head if he were successful, and Hades's helmet of invisibility. In order to get these items he first had to learn their whereabouts from the Graeae, sisters of the Gorgon who, between them possessed only one eye and one tooth with which to speak. Perseus crept up behind them and, at the moment that they exchanged the tooth and the

Above: With the help of the winged horse Pegasus, Perseus completed his adventures after overcoming the Gorgon Medusa.

Opposite: The Gorgon Medusa had offended the gods by invading the sacred temple of Athene, for which crime her hair was transformed into serpents, and her face turned all who looked upon her to stone.

Above: Vase decoration depicting Perseus slaying the Gorgon Medusa.

eye, he grabbed it and would not give it back until they had told him how to find the items he sought. He then collected these things from the Stygian Nymphs. He overcame the Gorgon by only looking at the beast in the reflection in his shield and cut off its head. Instantly, out of the body of the Gorgon appeared the winged horse Pegasus.

Carrying the Gorgon's head and mounted on Pegasus he headed back to claim his prize. On the way he first challenged, and beat, Atlas and turned him into a mountain. He wandered upon Andromeda, daughter of Cassiopeia, chained to a rock. He rescued her on the understanding that he would marry her. However her parents Cephaeus and Cassiopeia had no intention of honoring this once she was returned. Perseus was forced to turn them and all their court into stone using the Gorgon's head. Cephaeus and Cassiopeia became stars in the sky, but Andromeda later took a more important position in the heavens, as she married willingly.

Oedipus

Oedipus's father, Laius, King of Thebes and husband of Jocasta had been warned that not only would his son kill him but that the son would then marry his mother, Jocasta. In an attempt to thwart this prophecy, Laius took the infant to Mount Cithaeron, nailed his feet together and left him to die. The infant was saved by a shepherd and given the name Oedipus, because of the injuries to his feet. The shepherd then took Oedipus to Corinth where he was adopted by King Polybus.

When Oedipus reached manhood he received the full meaning of the original prophecy from the Delphic Oracle, and left Corinth to avoid his fate. He traveled to the city Thebes in Boeotia, but along the way met and fought with an old man.

Opposite: The Graeae were three old hags with only one eye and one tooth among them. They were tricked by Perseus into helping him to defeat Medusa.

Oedipus killed him, without realizing that it was his real father.

Guarding one of the roads entering the city of Thebes was the Sphinx who posed riddles to all travelers. Oedipus was the only one to answer correctly and with that, the Sphinx threw herself into the sea. Following the death of Laius, the new king Creon had ascended the throne and gave the crown and Jocasta in marriage to Oedipus, for defeating the Sphinx. Thus the second part of the prophecy came true. The couple had two sons and two daughters.

When Oedipus and Jocasta eventually learned of the terrible outcome of the original prophecy, Jocasta hanged herself and Oedipus blinded himself. Still this unfortunate family had not escaped the persisting hand of fate. Their sons eventually killed each other in a battle to determine the ruler of Thebes. Their daughter Antigone was buried alive by the Thebans as punishment for attending to her dead brother Polyneices, and her sister Iseme was buried with her. Of Oedipus there was very little more told. He wandered far afield, eventually settling in Attica, but effectively vanishing from the scene.

Io

Opposite: Oedipus defeated the Sphinx that guarded the roads into Thebes by answering the riddle, "What animal has four feet in the morning, two at midday, and three in the evening?"

The daughter of Inachus, king of Argos, Io was loved by Zeus. To keep her disguised from the vengeful eyes of Hera, Zeus turned her into a heifer. Hera discovered the ruse and set Argus, he of the hundred eyes, to guard her from Zeus. When Hermes killed Argus, Hera tormented Io with a gadfly that drove her across Europe and through Asia, until she was finally allowed to rest in Egypt. There Zeus returned her to human form, and she bore him a child called Epaphyus. Io has been identified with the Egyptian goddess Isis.

Right: Despite the duplicity and jealousy of Antaea, Bellerephon was successful in killing the fabled Chimera, with the help of the winged horse Pegasus.

Europa

The tale of Europa's abduction by Zeus is well-known. While she was picking flowers by the seashore one day, Zeus appeared to her in the form of a magnificent bull. Europa mounted the magnificent animal and Zeus made off with her across the sea to Crete. She gave birth to Minos, Rhadamanthus, and Sarpedon.

Cadmus

Cadmus was the son of Agenor and Telephassa and brother of Europa. Upon the abduction of his sister by Zeus, Cadmus set out with his two brothers to find her. On consulting the Oracle at Delphi he was advised to cease searching and build a city for Apollo. In order to do this he first had to kill the dragon at the spring of Ares and placed all the dragon's teeth in the ground. These teeth were transformed into warriors who then fought among themselves until

Left: One of the Muses with the severed head of Orpheus after he was torn to pieces by Thracian women. From a painting by Gustave Moreau.

only five remained. With Cadmus they built the city of Thebes.

Cadmus married Harmonia, the daughter of Ares and Aphrodite, and they had five children of whom Semele was later the mother of Dionysus, and Autonoe the mother of Acteon. Cadmus is credited with the "invention" of the alphabet.

Atalanta

Atalanta was born to Iasus but because he had always yearned for a son he dispatched her to the inhospitable slopes of Mount Parthenius. She did not perish, but was brought up by hunters and developed into an accomplished hunter and warrior.

She later slew two centaurs who had offended her and took part in many adventures. Her father, despite his earlier actions, eventually acknowledged her and decided that she should marry. Despising such an arrangement, Atalanta challenged all suitors to a race. If they lost, they would die. Melianon took up the awesome chal-

Right: Orpheus had the ability to charm even inanimate objects with the beauty of his music. Detail from a Roman sarcophagus.

Chapter Five

Roman Mythology

Roman mythology is heavily connected with that of the Greeks—indeed, many of the gods, goddesses, and heroes seem almost identical. Greek myths found their way into Roman civilization, where they were adapted to suit Roman culture, yet the rise of Rome from a small, pastoral settlement to perhaps the world's most successful empire is also one of the great epics of history and literature.

Jupiter

Jupiter was the king of the gods and of men. Also referred to under the name Jove, he was very similar in character and status to Zeus in the Greek legend. There was, however, far less emphasis on his amorous adventures. The Romans regarded him more as the god of light, their champion in battle, and the giver of victory. On the home front he was morally correct and the god of justice. As he was also connected with the important grape harvest, he was credited with command over the elements of weather including wind, rain, sunshine, thunder, and lightning.

Jupiter possessed three thunderbolts which he would use against man and particularly those who seemed intent upon wrong-doing. The dispatch of the first thunderbolt was intended as something of a warning shot to indicate his displeasure, the second was far more severe (suggesting the third was imminent), and the final bolt was fatal. It was rumored that for this final bolt to be dispatched Jupiter had to gain "permission" from certain unknown gods.

His statue appeared in all the most important locations and a temple was dedicated to Jupiter Optima Maximus on the Capitol. He was worshiped throughout Italy and, eventually, the Roman Empire.

Juno

Juno was the wife of Jupiter and queen of the gods. The stately and beautiful goddess of the moon and Heaven, she came to symbolize all the matronly qualities sought for in the Roman woman. She protected women not only in childbirth and rearing, but also in preparation for marriage and during the actual ceremony.

She also extended her protective influence over the whole city of Rome. When the Gauls attacked Rome, it was the sacred geese in the temple of Juno who alerted the defenders of the city and they were able to repulse the attack. The peacock was also dedicated to Juno. She was the Roman counterpart of Hera in Greek mythology, and, in certain aspects, shared something of the same character. Having been slightly put out by the unaided birth of Minerva (who sprang directly from the head of Jupiter), Juno contrived with Flora and she was fertilized by a mysterious flower and gave birth to Mars.

Mars

Mars was the rebellious son of Jupiter and Juno, and the Roman equivalent of Ares. He was the father of Romulus and Remus and, therefore, of very high regard among the Romans. Although he was the son of Juno, the belief that Jupiter was his father is in doubt. There was a tale that Mars's birth was aided by a fabulous flower (which might have been an excuse for unknown parentage) rather than by his mother's husband.

As with many other Roman gods before, and the influence of the Greek mythological history, Mars was first an agricultural deity and only later became the god of war. It is more precise to see Mars as the god of battles rather than general wars and the political causes which cause them to arise. He was worshiped prior to any military enterprise, and again during the battle, and offerings were made to him after a victory. Many of the stories related about his life are a retelling of those tales of Ares in Greek mythology.

He gave his name to the month of March and it was during that month that his sacred armor was carried through the streets of Rome by the priests. Chariot races would be held during this time and also at another festival in his name later in the year. These races were dedicated to Mars and it was traditional to sacrifice to him one of the horses from the winning team.

Vulcan

Son of Jupiter and Juno and, like Hephaestus in Greek mythology, Vulcan was the least physically prepossessing of the gods. He was the god of metal-working, fires, and the hearth. Vulcan was also the god of the thunderbolt which had been invented by Minerva, which he later gave to Jupiter. Vulcan was also the god of volcanoes, and his festival, the Volcanalia, was widely celebrated on August 23.

Opposite above: Seventeenth-century depiction of the great god Zeus (the Roman Jupiter), borne on a chariot and holding thunderbolts in one hand and the wand of office in the other.

Opposite below: A Gallic Vulcan. Carved on a Celtic monument under the choir of Notre-Dame, Paris.

Below: A Pompeiian household shrine depicting the head of the house, with two Lares (household gods) on either side. The Lares were protectors of domesticity and family life.

Right: Both Castor and Pollux were reputedly seen after the success of the Romans at the Battle of Regillus in 496 B.C., and were venerated in Rome from that time.

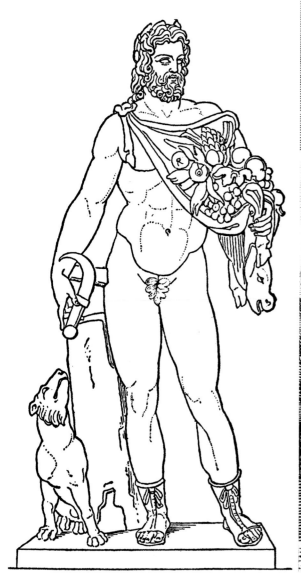

Above: Although taken from a print of 1904, this representation of the Roman god Silvanus shows him as less Pan-like than other depictions; he is bearing a cornucopia of fruits, the skin of an animal, and a sickle.

Opposite: A nineteenth-century representation of Mercury that includes all his various accoutrements: winged sandals and helmet, and the serpent-entwined staff.

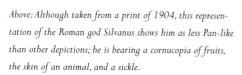

Mercury

Mercury was the son of Jupiter and Maia. He was the messenger of the gods and he fulfilled much the same function as Hermes did in Greece. In the role of messenger, he moved back and forth, delivering either entreaties or urgent warnings, between gods or directly to mortals. He appeared to Ulysses and gave good advice to him regarding Circe.

Carmenta, one of the nymphs known as the Camenae, was gifted with the power of prophecy. She had a son by Mercury, called Evander, during the time that she

Above: Mercury, the Roman counterpart of Hermes, delivering a message to Jupiter and Juno.

Opposite: Portunes (Palaemon in Greece), a sea god and son of Ino, was the Roman god of harbors. This Temple of Fortune was probably dedicated to him. He is often represented as a boy riding a dolphin.

lived in Attica in Greece. She later came to Italy with her son and is also credited with bringing with her the fifteen letters of the Greek alphabet.

Minerva

Minerva sprang from Jupiter's head and had no mother. Her plant was the olive, and the owl was her symbolic animal, both of which she shares with Athene.

Minerva was equal in importance and popularity with Jupiter and Juno in Roman mythology. Minerva shared many of the qualities of the Greek Athene, particularly in the manner of her birth. She is claimed to have burst forth from the head of Jupiter, fully armed. Patroness of the arts and crafts and goddess of wisdom, Minerva is also credited with the invention of the thunderbolt, but this she gave to Vulcan.

Saturn

Saturn was the Roman god of agriculture and crops whose symbol was the scythe. Saturn is identified with Cronus in Greek mythology and his exploits were very similar. He too consumed his children but, in his case, it was all but three of them—Pluto, Jupiter, and Neptune. Each of these represented the grave, the air and water, and it was believed that none of these three could be consumed by time, in other words, by Saturn.

Saturn was the god of agricultural abundance and plenty, and the Feast of Saturnalia was in his honor. Held for seven days starting on the December 19th, the feast was extremely popular with the Romans, not least for its lack of restraint. Making merry and overindulging were the prime requirements. No public offices

Above: Of ancient origin, Fortuna represented fate.
Representations of her always stood in the sleeping quarters
of the emperors, and those who were lucky in public office
were said to "possess a Fortuna."

were open, no official business conducted and slaves were served by their masters. The Festival ended on December 23rd.

Vesta

The Roman version of the Greek Hestia, Vesta symbolized fire and light and became the goddess of the home and, particularly, the hearth. The sacred flame in her temple in the Regia in Rome was brought by Aeneas from Troy and was never allowed to be extinguished. It was tended by the Vestal Virgins.

Vestal Virgins were chosen from the patrician, upper class families of Rome and served for thirty years. They took vows of absolute chastity and any deviation from this was severely punished. In the early days their crimes consisted of being whipped to death. But this was later changed to being whipped and then walled up alive. There was also another crime in addition to the breaking of the chastity law. If they were in attendance at any time when the sacred flame died, they would be put to death by whipping. Despite these dire penalties for falling short of expectations. they otherwise enjoyed a good life. This is further born out by the fact that the majority of Vestal Virgins continued with their duties long after they were officially allowed to leave and marry. In over a thousand years of their profession only about twenty ever quit.

Janus

Janus is one of the Roman gods for whom there is no direct equivalent in the myths of the Greeks, and the god who, misguidedly gave us the expression "being two-faced." Janus was the two-faced god, not in any derogatory sense, but because he was the deity in charge of doorways and entrances, all of which have two sides.

He gave his name to the month of January—being the month at the "entrance" of the year. He could then look backwards into the old year and forward to the new. The doors of the temple of Janus in the Forum in Rome were always open in times of war and closed during peaceful periods.

Left: The two-faced God Janus, guardian of doorways, the old and new year, and keeper of the gate of Heaven.

Following pages: The Temple of Apollo at Rhodes, largest of the Dodecanese Isles.

Above: The Roman Mother Earth, Ceres, was the goddess of nature and agriculture. From a mosaic at Cirencester, England.

Diana

Diana was the huntress and goddess of the moon. The equivalent of the Roman Artemis, Diana was the protectress of woodland, hunters, and conversely, wild animals, as well as women in childbirth. At her temple on the Aventine at Rome she was honored as the virgin goddess. Diana was also instrumental in saving Hippolytus from further destruction from his mother Phaedra when she deluded his father Theseus. She removed him to Italy and placed him in the more tender care of a nymph.

Ceres

Ceres was the daughter of Saturn and the Roman counterpart of Demeter in Greek myths. Her daughter was Prosperine who later became Pluto's wife. She is noted for her curse upon Erisichthon. He was a very unpleasant person who tried to chop down an oak tree dedicated by the woodland nymphs to the Goddess Ceres. Despite all protestations by the nymphs, Erisichthon attacked the tree with an ax, and even when the tree bled, he continued. Ceres then sent for the goddess Famine to possess Erisichthon. He was consequently so consumed with hunger that nothing could satisfy him. He sold his daughter repeatedly in order to buy food and eventually consumed his own body.

Bacchus

Bacchus was the son of Jupiter, and the Roman god of wine. Worship of Bacchus was often an excuse for excessive behavior and it was banned by the Roman Senate in 186 B.C. Although relegated in importance to that of a "mystery" cult, it gained popularity again in the first centuries after Christ.

Left: Diana, an ancient Italian goddess with many of the attributes of the Greek Artemis. She was mainly worshiped by women in Roman society.

Above: The baby Dionysus (the Roman Bacchus) being transported in a chariot. From a Roman mosaic in Paphos, Cyprus.

Venus

Venus was the daughter of Jupiter from his liaison with Dione. She was the goddess of love, the Roman equivalent of the Greek Aphrodite, and is the namesake of a variety of plants, planets, and physical attributes. While we often assume that she was one of the most important Roman gods, she was, in fact, something of a late comer to the scene. She was worshiped in the Roman world but, despite the fame of her physical attributes, she commenced life as one of the "agricultural" divinities.

As in the Greek tales, she was reputed to have been born of the sea foam and married Vulcan (Hephaestus) but continued with her ability to charm other men.

One day, while playing with her son Cupid, she was scratched by one of his arrows. The cut was far deeper than she suspected and it had its effect. The first person she saw after that was Adonis. She fell so in love with him that all other matters in her life were forgotten. She even joined Adonis in his favorite pastime of hunting. Despite her warnings regarding the savagery of the hunt Adonis pursued, and wounded, a wild boar with his spear. The boar turned on Adonis and fatally gored him. Even though Venus returned to the dying Adonis as quickly as she

could, he died. Where the drops of his blood fell, the dark red anemone flower grew.

In the time of Imperial Rome, Venus was worshiped as Venus Genetrix, mother of Aeneas, Venus Felix, the bringer of good fortune, and Venus Verticordia, protector of feminine chastity.

Above: Edward Burne-Jones's painting The Mirror of Venus *bears a strong allusion to the passage in* The Golden Bough *referring to the Mirror of Diana. In that instance, the "mirror" was a lake in the Alban Hills, Aricia, Italy.*

Cupid

The son of Venus, and the Roman counterpart of the Greek Eros, Cupid is always depicted as a young boy with wings, a bow, and arrows. He was more a mischievous urchin than a model of family rectitude. He laughed at the facial distortions of Minerva as she attempted to play the flute and delighted in mischievous acts concerning the hearts of both gods and mortals.

However, Cupid himself fell in love with the beautiful maiden Psyche. Psyche had incurred Venus's jealousy by unwittingly attracting attention from the followers of the cult of Venus, and she commanded her son Cupid to use his powers so that

117

Above: Cupid and Psyche. Despite the heartlessness of Venus towards her, Psyche (the epitome of the soul) was finally reunited with her lover, Cupid (Eros in Greek myth).

Psyche would be attracted to the basest, meanest, and most unworthy mortal she laid eyes on. Cupid did his work and pierced Psyche's flesh with an arrow. But in waking Psyche they both realized their mutual attraction.

A very jealous and annoyed Venus then set numerous difficult tasks for the unfortunate Psyche. Her final task was to descend to the kingdom of Pluto and return with the box belonging to Prosperine. This had to remain unopened, as it contained, according to Venus, all the beauty of the goddesses. Psyche did as she was commanded but, out of curiosity, opened the box. Immediately the perpetual sleep contained within the box escaped and Psyche fell into a deathless sleep. Cupid then flew to Jupiter and pleaded for his help. Psyche was taken up into the realm of the gods and the marriage between Cupid and Psyche became, in the eyes of the gods, immortal.

Flora

Opposite: Flora, the Roman goddess of flowers and fertility. Her Festival of Floralia was held between April 28 and May 8.

The goddess of flowers who, in early Roman forms was also the goddess of the spring, new shoots and crops, Flora was frequently invoked during the burgeoning season early in the year to propitiate over the coming crops. The Festival of Floralia

STATUE DU DIEU SILVAIN

(yet another excuse for the Romans to enjoy the fruits of their existence) ran from April 21st into the first weeks of May. It is also interesting to note that the French also had a similar festival—the Floreal (the month of flowers) during the eighth month of the revolutionary calendar.

Opposite: Silvanus was a woodland and forest god, protector of cattle. He was the product of the union of Sybaris, a shepherd, and a she-goat, and often confused with Pan or Faunus.

Faunus

Faunus was a god and, reputedly, the grandson of Saturn and son of Picus. He ruled over the fields and shepherds and his name was used for the class of woodland deities known as fawns. Faunus appears under differing names throughout Roman mythology but most recognizably as the god Pan (a name which was retained from the Greek equivalent) and also as Silvanus (a fertility god and one of the earliest to enter Roman lore as a "rustic" god).

In addition to overseeing day-to-day agricultural work and fertility of the soil he also had an unnerving ability to make voices heard in the countryside. Of his several names, Lupercus is interesting. A temple was erected on the original site of the founding of Rome, the Palatine hill. On February 15th of each year the Festival of Lupercalia was celebrated. (St. Valentine's Day is the now the nearest approximation we have today to this Roman feast.) Lupercalia was a feast of purification and women who wished to become pregnant were brought to the fore during the ceremonies.

Faunus had a daughter (or, in some versions, a wife or sister) called Fauna who, while being a protectress and goddess of fertility and crops, was celebrated in a festival during December. This was a very strictly women-only event and the proceedings are shrouded in mystery, but are reputed to have ended in an orgy on each occasion.

Left: The statue of Romulus and Remus, which graces the Capitoline Hill, Rome. The Capitoline Hill was the most important of the Seven Hills of Rome, and the site of the main temples and ancient citadel.

Previous pages: A beautiful Roman mosaic from Herculaneaum, depicting Neptune and his wife, Amphitrite.

Romulus and Remus

Romulus and Remus were the twin sons of the union between Mars, the God of War, and the mortal Rhea Silvia. Rhea Silvia was, in turn, the daughter of Numitor, the king of Alba Longa, the city later called Latium southeast of modern Rome. She was either persuaded, or forced, to become a Vestal Virgin by her uncle Amulius who had deposed her father from the throne.

After Silvia bore Romulus and Remus, Amulius imprisoned Silvia and cast the two infants into the River Tiber. They were eventually washed ashore, suckled by a she-wolf and a woodpecker (both sacred to the god Mars) and then cared for by herdsmen. When they reached manhood they exacted revenge upon Amulius, killing him and restoring Numitor to his rightful throne.

They then built Rome, but not without a bitter dispute regarding its actual site, in which Romulus killed Remus. Romulus is also held responsible for the infamous act known as the Rape of the Sabine women. As Rome was reputedly built by men alone, (or, more likely, that the builders and early dwellers were thieves and vagabonds with whom no right-minded Roman woman would associate), Romulus led the men on a expedition against the Sabine tribe to supply women to the city. It was only following the decision by the Sabine women to actually stay in Rome despite their abduction, that a major war was averted.

Romulus vanished from the scene many years afterward, and, according to certain Roman historians, he ascended Mount Olympus and became a god.

Opposite: An eighteenth-century depiction of Romulus fixing the actual site for the city of Rome. It was during this event that a quarrel broke out between Romulus and Remus, which resulted in the death of Remus.

Below: Romulus and Remus, in modern times, have come to symbolize the spirit of ancient Rome.

Index

Page numbers in boldface indicate photos.

Acteon 56, 97
Admete 83
Adonis 60, 116, 117
Aeetes, King 87, 91
Aegeus, King 86, 87
Aeneas 60, 110
Aeson, King 87
Aethra 36, 86
Agenor 96
Agrigento 9, 40
Agrisius, King 91
Alcippe 43
Alcmena 79
Alcyone 61
Amaltheia 23
Amazons 81, 83, 87
Amphitrite 36, 120–121
Amphitryon 79
Amulius 125
Anchises 59
Andromeda 93
Antaeus 36, 84
Antigone 34, 94
Antiope 87
Aphaeia 66
Aphrodite 13, 19, 25, 34, 43–44, 57, 59, 60, 71, 73, 76
  see also Venus; baths of 44; Rocks of 20–21
Apollo 25, 46, 49, 49, 53–54, 56, 58, 64, 79, 96;
  temples 23, 26–27, 46, 48, 52, 62–63, 76, 112–113
Arachne 66–67
Ares 25, 28, 34, 42–44, 60, 71, 73 see also Mars
Arges 18
Argo 66, 87, 91
Argonauts 87, 91
Argus 94
Ariadne 86, 87
Arion 36, 38
Aristaeus 101
Artemis 25, 53, 54–57, 59, 79 see also Diana
Asclepius 53
Atalanta 97, 101
Athamas, King 64, 87
Athene 25, 29, 43, 45, 66–67, 67, 84, 91 see also Minerva;
  temples of 7, 65, 67
Atlas 61, 70, 93
Atropos 77
Augean Stables 83
Autonoe 97

Bacchus 115
Bellerephon 96, 101
Benthesicyme 36
Blessed, Isles of the 9, 69
Boreas 9, 17
Briarius 18
Brontes 18

Cadmus, King 31, 96, 97
Calliope 29, 101
Callisto 56
Camenae 106

Capotoline Hill 123
Carmenta 106
Cassiopeia 93
Castor 106
Cedalion 45–46
Celoeno 61
Centaurs 61, 84, 87
Cephaeus 93
Cerberus 81, 84, 84
Ceres 114, 115
Cermenta 108
Chaos 17
Charon 68
Chimera 101
Chiron 87
Chryse 44
Circe 71, 72
Clio 29
Clotho 77
Coeus 18, 46
Constellations 9, 34, 36, 56–57, 61, 93, 101
Corinth 48
Coronis 53
Cottus 18
Creation 17
Creon, King 81, 94
Cretan Bull 83
Crius 18
Cronus 18–19, 22, 22–23 see also Saturn
Crows 53
Cupid 116–118, 118
Cycnus 44
Cyniras, King 60
Cyrene 101

Danae 91
Daphne 49, 49, 53
Deimos 43
Deimus 44, 60
Delos, Island of 49, 50–51
Delphi 9, 22, 23, 26–27, 46, 47, 54, 58, 76, 94;
  Oracle at 81, 91, 93, 96
Demeter 22, 25, 38, 39–40, 41 see also Ceres
Deucalion 101
Diana 114, 115
Dice 28, 77
Dicte, Mount 23
Dike 29
Diomedes 84
Dione 25, 57, 59, 116
Dionysus 25, 31, 31, 59, 60, 64, 116 see also Bacchus
  Ear of 60
Dragon's teeth 91, 96, 97

Echo 57
Eirene 29
Electra 61
Eleusis 39
Endymion 73
Enyo 43
Eos 25, 69, 69, 73, 76 see also Aurora
Epaphyus 94

Erato 29
Erichthonius 67
Eris 43
Erisichthon 115
Eros 55 see also Cupid
Erymanthian Boar 83
Eryx 84
Ethiopeans 9
Eumenides 78, 81
Eunomia 28–29, 77
Euphemis 36
Europa 36, 96
Eurydice 101
Eurynome 29, 45
Eurystheus 82–84
Eurytion 84
Eurytus 84
Euterpe 29
Evander 106, 108

Famine 115
Fates see Moerae
Fauna 123
Faunus 123
Floods 101
Flora 104, 118, 119
Floralia 118, 123
Flowers 53, 60, 117
Fortuna 110
Fortune see Portunes
Fountains 12, 37
Furies see Eumenides

Gaea 17–19, 23, 36, 66
Ganymede 28, 77
Garden of the Hesperides 13
Geryon 84
Girdle of the Amazons 81, 83
Glacus 101
Golden Apples of the Hesperides 84
Golden Fleece 87, 87, 91
Gorgon see Medusa
Graces 28–29
Graeae 91, 92, 93
Great Mother 17
Gyges 18

Hades 22, 25, 28, 38, 41, 64, 84, 101 see also Pluto
Halirrhothius 43
Harmonia 44, 60, 97
Hebe 28, 34, 77
Hecate 28
Hele 87
Helen of Troy 59
Helios 25, 69, 71–73
Hephaestus 13, 25, 28–29, 34, 43–46, 67, 71 see also
  Vulcan
Hera 22, 25, 28, 30–34, 34, 45–46, 49, 59, 64, 64, 77,
  79, 81, 83–84, 94 see also Juno; temples 6, 30, 30, 32–33
Heracles 43, 77, 79, 79, 81; Labors of 81–84;
  Pillars of 84
Hermaphroditus 60
Hermes 25, 56, 58, 60–61, 64, 66 see also Mercury

Picture Credits